FIRESTORM

FIRESTORM

MAURINE H. GEE
illustrated by Charles Geer

SCHOLASTIC BOOK SERVICES
NEW YORK · TORONTO · LONDON · AUCKLAND · SYDNEY · TOKYO

Copyright © 1968 by Maurine H. Gee. This edition is published by Scholastic Book Services,
division of Scholastic Magazines, Inc., by arrangement with William Morrow & Company, In

3rd printing .... January 1974

Printed in the U.S.A.

CONTENTS

BO-THE-CROW

The swimming pool shone blue and inviting behind the big white house with its thick adobe walls and red-tiled roof. The land in back of the house sloped gently to the floor of Rosario Canyon in a series of terraces planted to fruit trees and avocados. The swimming pool was on the upper level flanked by a cabana with four dressing rooms.

At sight of the pool and the tall fiber-glass slide that towered against the blue sky Ken Marr could scarcely resist making a dash for it, clothes and all. It was the only pool on this side of the canyon. Ken and his best friend, Cubby Conners, who had lived on the north rim of the canyon all their eleven years, knew how lucky they were to have Merv Hollis ask them over for a swim.

That slide by the pool brought out the seal in Ken. There was a breathtaking dip in it, and a trickle of water to keep it wet and slippery. The slide was high, it was fast, and it was scary.

"Yippee!" Ken shouted on his first trip down. "Watch the big splash."

He could never get enough of the slide. First the slick wet cement of the poolside underfoot, then his bare toes curled around the chrome treads of the ladder. The pause at the top of the slide to let the thrill of near panic sink in. Then the belly flop and the head-first flight down the slippery dips to the water. Down, down through the tingling rush of water until one outstretched hand touched the bottom.

"This is the greatest," he called to Merv, when he came up for air.

Cubby kept heckling until he got Ken to race Merv from one end of the pool to the other. As judge, Cubby kept yelling instructions to both of them all the way. The race ended in a tie.

"You'll have to try again," Cubby shouted.

"I won," yelled Merv.

"No, I won," yelled Ken.

Merv tried to duck him, and they were both underwater when Cubby pulled Merv to the surface. "Hey, Merv," he shouted. "Your mother wants you."

Mrs. Hollis had come out on the balcony that overlooked the gardens. Her hair was in big fat rollers, and she clutched a white terry-cloth robe around her.

"Yoo hoo, Mervin," she called. "I left my new bifocal glasses down there on the table. Please put them in the house on my desk before they get broken."

"Will do," Merv shouted, and he dived under the water dragging Ken down with him.

Ken stayed down and held his breath as long as possible. When he came up he saw that Merv and Cubby were staring at a large magnolia tree near the pool.

"Hey, Ken," Cubby yelled, "it's your crazy bird, Bo-the-crow. He's afraid he's missing out on something."

Bo glided down from the magnolia tree and strode across the grass toward them. He moved with a proud, rolling walk, his head bobbing back and forth at every step.

"He struts like a bowlegged sailor," said Merv.

Bo paused in his march long enough to make a dive for something in the grass. He braced himself and tried to pull an angleworm from its burrow. The worm stretched out like a tough rubber band. Bo had a real tussle before he managed to gobble it down.

He wiped his beak on the grass and hurried on toward the pool, apparently feeling he had neglected his duty by taking time out for a snack. In his hurry to regain lost time he began to hop across the grass on both feet as though he were on a pogo stick.

"Look at that clown," cried Cubby, and he laughed so hard he slipped on the wet cement and took a dive into the water.

Jauntily Bo soared to a perch on the back of a black-and-white chair. "What's new?" he intoned. "What's new?"

Merv crouched down and pretended to sneak up on him. "Meow," he teased. "Meow."

"Save your strength," Ken said. "He'll never let you get near."

He was right. Bo quickly looked over the clutter on the table beside him. Before anyone knew what he was up to, he dived at the table and went flying off with the pair of glasses, which had pretty sparkly stones on the bows.

"Mom's glasses," Merv shouted. He made a desperate lunge at Bo, but the crow was too fast for him.

"Oh, no," cried Ken.

Merv turned on him flushed with anger. "Do something," he yelled, giving Ken a shove that almost knocked him down. "He's your bird. You've got to get those glasses. What's my mother going to say when she finds out I forgot about her glasses? I'm dead, that's what."

"Chasing Bo won't do any good," said Ken.

"Remember the time he stole my dad's car keys?" said Cubby. "No one ever saw them again."

Merv waved Ken on his way. "Don't just stand there," he said.

Ken knew that chasing after Bo was silly. The bird never flew straight to his hideaway when he made off with something. He always took the long way home so no one would discover its location. Gingerly Ken ran down the driveway to the street, the gravel biting into his bare feet. He didn't care about his clothes or his towel or his shoes. He only knew that Merv was sore and he no longer felt welcome.

Shortly after Ken arrived home, the telephone began to ring. It was Merv Hollis. Ken clutched the receiver tightly.

"What's on your mind?" he asked cautiously.

"I'm calling for my mother," said Merv coolly. "She's coming down there to speak to your mother, and she wants to be sure you'll be home."

Ken sensed a threat. "Sounds like you're trying to get me in bad," he said.

"You'll find out," said Merv, as though he were an adult speaking to a two-year-old. "We'll be there soon as Mother finishes dressing."

Ken replaced the receiver and hurried outside. He found his mother cutting roses for the house.

"We're going to have company," he told her. "Mrs. Hollis is coming down here to see you."

Mrs. Marr looked startled. "Oh dear, look at me. My shoes all muddy and no face on."

"Could be she wants to see me," Ken admitted.

"You!" Mrs. Marr stared. "Are you in some kind of trouble?"

Ken squirmed. "I hope not," he said, and certainly that was the truth.

His mother hurriedly motioned him back to the house. "Here, take these roses and put them in the blue vase on the kitchen sink. I want them on the coffee table in the living room."

Ken took the thorny bunch of fragrant flowers. He didn't mind getting punctured by thorns, but he did mind facing the callers.

When his mother started upstairs, she paused on the landing to call to him. "Be sure to answer the doorbell if the Hollises get here before I come down."

Ken ran after her. "What do I say?" he protested. "What do I do?"

"Invite them in and see that they are seated," said Mrs. Marr. "I'll be right down."

Ken didn't waste much time on the flowers. He

managed to get them on the coffee table without mishap, and then he began to listen for the sound of the Hollis car in the driveway. He had moved from the sofa to the green-and-gold striped chair a dozen times before the car drove in.

His hand was sweaty on the knob as he opened the front door. There before him stood Mrs. Hollis wearing a hat and white gloves. Even Merv was all slicked up with his hair freshly combed.

Regarding Ken as though they were strangers, he handed him the clothes that had been left in the cabana. "Here's the stuff you left at my house," he said stiffly. "And this is my mother, Mrs. Hollis."

Ken said he was glad to meet her—the misstatement of the year—and led the way to the living room and the striped chair.

Mrs. Hollis seated herself and smiled pleasantly as though she were very sure of herself with young people. "What a lovely house," she said. She looked around the room and let her glance linger on the roses. "They come from your garden, don't they?" she asked. "I noticed the large circular bed as we drove in."

Ken could think of nothing to add to that remark.

To his relief, however, his mother appeared in the doorway. He got to his feet, hoping this next part was going to come off properly.

"Mrs. Hollis," he said, "I want you to meet my mother, Mrs. Marr."

The women smiled and exchanged greetings. Mrs. Marr sat in the chair opposite Mrs. Hollis, and they got in a lot of smooth talk about gardening and sprays before Mrs. Hollis came to the reason for her visit.

"I didn't come to borrow a cup of sugar," she said with a smile. "And I know it's bad form to move to a new neighborhood and start criticizing. But there's one thing I'd like to mention. I left a pair of glasses on the table beside our swimming pool today, and your son's pet crow made off with them."

"Oh, I'm so sorry," cried Mrs. Marr in quick sympathy. She turned to Ken. "Did you know about this?"

Ken nodded. "Could be," he admitted.

Mrs. Hollis got to her feet. "I had no idea we were moving into a neighborhood of delinquent crows," she said, still smiling. "The glasses were bifocals in expensive frames, so I've told Mervin if they aren't found he and the boys will not use the pool for a week."

Merv glared coldly at Ken.

"Well now, Mrs. Hollis," Ken's mother said, "I'm sorry about this. Ken, you go out to Bo's nest and look for those glasses."

"You go with him," Mrs. Hollis told Merv. "I'm sure you can help."

Ken didn't want anything to do with that sorehead. It didn't seem fair to Bo to let Merv know the location of his hideaway.

Silently Merv followed Ken along the driveway and across the street to the towering eucalyptus windbreak that faced the house. They saw nothing of Bo until they started to climb his special tree. Then he appeared flapping overhead with a low chuckling caw that was meant as a friendly warning to cease and desist. However, when they paid no attention, his tone changed to a loud indignant cawing. He seemed determined to warn the entire neighborhood that poachers were on the loose.

When Ken reached the abandoned tree house with its warped flooring and its palm-thatched roof, Merv was right there behind him breathing down his neck.

"Move on up," Merv said. "I'd like to have a look around."

Ken pulled himself to a sitting position on a splintery floorboard, and Merv peered in at the faded blue canvas backrest, the rickety orange crate, and the rusty green tea kettle that Ken and his friends had once used. Next to the orange crate was a collection of sticks, string, leaves, roots, and dry grass with a few black feathers scattered around to mark the place as Bo's home. All around, inside and outside the nest, Bo had stored his collection of bright treasures. There were shiny discs that had once been the tops of tin cans, pieces of broken glass, a tinsel star, a pinkish shell, and a silvery gum wrapper. Ken sorted through it all, but there were no glasses.

Bo had perched on a nearby limb, where he sat complaining loudly in crow talk. Merv made a movement to shoo him away.

"Boy, if I had a gun that bird would sure stop his squawking."

"You can't shoot a gun around here," Ken stated flatly. "Not even on your own property. It's illegal."

"I've heard that one," said Merv.

Ken shook his head. "I'm not joking. It's against the law to shoot a gun in this canyon."

Merv scowled. "Look, I know I'm new here and all

that but I'm not dumb. With my own ears just this morning I heard shots down there in the canyon. I heard them plain as could be."

"Oh, that," said Ken. "That was the exterminator. He traps coyotes and then shoots them."

Merv turned to leave. "You're never going to find those glasses," he said in disgust. "Now we can't use the pool! I still say that bird ought to be shot."

He climbed down the crosspieces and kicked up a storm of eucalyptus leaves as he crossed to the road.

CLUB MEETING

After school the next day Ken walked up the hill from the bus stop with Cubby and Merv. Merv seemed resigned today to his loss of pool privileges. He pointed toward a dark smoke cloud that billowed up beyond the mountain ridge to the north.

"I thought people weren't allowed to burn trash around here," he said.

"They're not," said Ken. "That must be a brush fire over in Tortugas Canyon. When it's this dry, spot fires break out, but the firemen go right after them."

"Wait till we get a dry hot wind from the Mojave Desert," said Cubby, "then you'll see some real action." He ran the back of his hand across his mouth. "My lips feel chapped just thinking about it."

"He means a Santa Ana wind," said Ken. "We only get a few of them each year, but then everyone thinks of fire."

"If it's so dangerous," said Merv, "why do people build houses in canyons?"

Ken shrugged. "We're not down in the canyon, we're up on the rim of the canyon where we can see all around. What could be nicer than the mountains on one side, the ocean on the other, and no neighbors in back?"

"The nicest thing about Rosario Canyon," said Cubby, "is that we never have fires."

Merv gave him a mocking look. "Oh, sure," he said. "Every canyon has fires except ours."

"It's true," Ken assured him. He picked up a stick and half knelt at the side of the road where the macadam gave way to decomposed granite. He brushed the gravel smooth and drew a large horseshoe. "Let's say this horseshoe is our canyon," he said. "Both sides run east and west." He studded the horseshoe outline with pieces of gravel. "These rocks are the houses. The far side is the South Rim and our side is the North Rim." He drew in a series of wavy parallel lines. "Down here at the mouth of the horseshoe is the

Pacific. There seems to be something about the lay of the land that keeps the fires away from us. Don't ask me what it is, ask some meteorologist. There are canyons like ours all along the coast, and most of them have had their fires. But Rosario Canyon hasn't had a fire that any of the old-timers can remember."

"It's true," said Cubby happily. "We've never had trouble here."

Ken got up and dusted off his knee, but he could see that he had not got through to Merv.

When they reached Ken's own white, green-roofed house, his dog Mugsy came charging out to meet him. Ken braced himself for the impact. Mugsy, half Chesapeake Bay retriever and half American foxhound, weighed sixty pounds or more, and he thought nothing of bowling Ken over to show his love and affection.

Ken managed to stay on his feet. "Atta boy," he said, turning his face aside to avoid a wet kiss. "Down, boy. Sit!"

Merv stood there eying Mugsy with a critical squint. "What is he?" he asked, as though Mugsy were a three-legged rooster or something.

Ken hesitated, but Cubby spoke right up. "He's a new breed," he said proudly. "He's a cross between a champion American foxhound and a champion Chesapeake retriever."

"Quite a mixture," said Merv. He turned to Ken. "What's the name of this new breed?"

Ken sensed that Merv was trying to lead him on, trying to find something to ridicule. "I haven't decided," he said.

"He thinks maybe he'll call it a Cheshund," said Cubby. "Sort of a combination of Chesapeake and hound."

Merv's eyebrows went up in mock agreement. "Ah, a Cheesehound," he said, deliberately stressing the first syllable. "He chases cheese. Right?"

Ken went along with the sour joke. "Sure," he said. "He even chases his own tail."

"My dog's a champion," Merv said in a superior tone. "He's an Afghan hound. Tops as a hunter. Abdul tracks by sight instead of smell."

"Don't worry, Old Mugsy is plenty smart," said Cubby. "Ken's training him to retrieve, so when he goes dove hunting with his dad they can take Mugsy along."

Ken wished Cubby would pipe down. He hated to have his poor mixed-up Mugsy compared to a dog like

Merv's. "See you later," he said abruptly. "I've got to work Mugsy. He probably forgot a lot since our last session."

Merv started up the road. "Some hunting dog," he said with a smile. "Come on, Cubby, let's go."

Mugsy started to follow them. Ken's voice was harsh as he called him back. Having his best friend trail off after Merv was bad enough without having his dog go too.

He shut Mugsy in the storage room off the garage while he went to the house to get his poultry bait. He found his sister, Crissy, on the back porch polishing a pair of brown-and-white shoes. She glanced suspiciously at him, and asked, "What's that terrible smell out here?" Crissy was sixteen and considered Ken too young to have good sense.

Ken shrugged. "Probably an old fish can," he said. He put his books down and began to look under a pile of newspapers. At last he brought out a lumpy brown paper bag.

"That's it," cried his sister. "Whew! What's in there?"

Ken opened the rumpled bag, and even he was staggered by the ripe smell. "They're duck wings with the

feathers left on," he said. "I got them at the poultry
market to help teach Mugsy to retrieve."

"Get them out of here," cried Crissy. "They smell
terrible."

"To a dog they smell great," Ken said. He poked
the open sack under her nose, and she reeled back a
step.

"Don't tell me you're going to poison Mugsy with
that rotten meat," she protested.

"He's not going to eat any. The idea is to hide them
and make him find them. That teaches him to have a
keen nose."

"Those are enough to ruin his smeller forever," said Crissy.

Ken took his bait outside. He tied a string to two of the wings and pulled them over the grass to the potting shed, where he hid the wings beside a bag of fertilizer. He figured Mugsy would develop a pretty good nose if he could learn to smell those wings when they were near something as strong as the fertilizer. The other two wings he hid under a mountain lilac bush that grew near the rim of the canyon.

When he freed Mugsy from the storage room, he let him smell the stiff paper sack. "Seek!" he ordered. "Seek!"

Mugsy cocked his head and looked at Ken with big reddish brown eyes that held a puzzled expression.

"Oh, no," said Ken with a groan. "Don't tell me you've forgotten again."

He gave Mugsy another smell of the sack. Then he got down on all fours and began to demonstrate how the search should proceed. He sniffed loudly along the trail that the smelly wings had left.

"Seek!" he commanded sternly. "Seek!"

Mugsy pretended to get the idea. He sidled along beside Ken and sniffed at the back of Ken's neck,

trying to appear busy. This act was all a big bluff. With a great deal of coaching he finally sniffed out the first two wings, though he didn't seem properly excited over his find.

Mrs. Marr came out in the garden to work among the chrysanthemums.

"Sometimes I think Mugsy just plays dumb to get out of work," Ken told her.

"Could be," she agreed pleasantly. "I know a certain boy who tries the same trick."

Friday afternoon five boys filed into Mrs. Marr's potting shed. Vic Ward hitched up his high-water pants and seated himself on a half sack of leaf mold. Ron Austin backed up to the aluminum ladder and sat on the lower step, his elbows resting on his knees. Harvey Bushnell peered around from under his shaggy mop of dark hair and chose an unopened sack of fertilizer for his perch. Ken took the seat of honor on the red wheelbarrow and motioned for Cubby to be seated beside him.

Ken reached for a trowel on the potting bench and tapped on a flower pot for attention. "The meeting of the North Rim Protective Club for Pets and Wildlife will come to order," he said, referring to some notes he had written on the back of an envelope. "Cubby, let's have the roll call."

Cubby took a little notebook from his hip pocket and read off the names of all those present. He got a response from everyone until he called out the name of Benjie Hardesty.

"He's excused," said Ken. "He had to go to the dentist to get his braces tightened."

"Okay," said Cubby. "That leaves you and me, and we're all present except Benjie."

Ken nodded. "We won't bother with the treasurer's report on account of we haven't collected any dues," he said. He motioned to Cubby. "Go ahead with the minutes of the previous meeting."

Cubby stood up and read from his notes. "At the last meeting we voted to drop the fifty-cent membership fee until further notice. Our president agreed to write a letter to the U.S. Fish and Wildlife Service, or whoever is boss of our canyon, and get them to stop that exterminator from setting out coyote traps that end up crippling our dogs. And that takes care of the previous meeting."

Cubby sat down, and Ken glanced at the other three members. "Any corrections?" he asked.

Vic Ward cleared his throat. "You left out about the cats," he told Cubby. "That letter was to read dogs *and* cats."

"Aw, cats are too smart to get caught in a trap," said Ron Austin.

An argument started, and Ken tapped the clay pot. "Don't worry," he said. "In the letter I said both dogs and cats. Not only that, but I used my dad's typewriter and his business stationery when I wrote it. That's why we got such a fast reply." He took an envelope from his pocket and handed it to Cubby. "Will the secretary please read the letter?"

Ken had taken the letter to school that day. Although he had showed it to each of the club members, none had been allowed to read it.

"Well," said Cubby, "you all know the letter is from the Animal Regulation Department. It starts off with the date, and then it goes on, 'Dear Sir: We try to make it clear that our coyote-trapping programs are designed to safeguard the pets of hillside residents while reducing an overpopulation of predators. Despite a protest or two from wildlife conservationists, we must continue to trap dangerous animals. We do not plan to drive the coyote to extinction, but merely to restore the balance of nature. Yours sincerely, Nevin Sorenson, District Supervisor for the Animal Regulation Department.' "

"Sounds like they're going to keep right on setting out those traps," said Vic Ward.

"Sure does," Ken agreed. "You notice Mr. Sorenson just skips over all we had to say about the trapper using varmint scent and varmint callers that sound like a wounded rabbit and those flashlights."

"I said we were wasting our time," Harvey Bushnell chimed in. "What do those guys care about our dogs getting caught in traps?"

"Well, anyway, we tried to be fair," said Ron Austin. "We gave them their chance. I vote we save the letter. If we get in trouble, we can prove we wrote them."

"Second the motion," said Harvey.

Ken nodded. "There's nothing left for us to do but to return to our usual Saturday plan. We'll meet here tomorrow morning at nine thirty. Ron, you tell Benjie our plans, but don't breathe a word to anyone else. Not anyone. Especially Merv Hollis. I don't trust him."

"Fair enough," said Cubby. "We'll be here tomorrow at nine thirty."

Ken stood to one side as his friends filed out of the potting shed. "See you tomorrow for the Saturday special," he told each one of them. "Don't forget your bows and arrows."

THE SATURDAY SPECIAL

Ken was glad to see Saturday roll around. By nine thirty he was sure he had every chore attended to, and yet his mother called to him before he could get out the back door.

"I hear water running," she said. "I can hear it in the pipes."

"Maybe it's in the bathroom," said Ken.

"No, I checked," she said. "Look around outside."

Ken found the running water all right. The night before, Mugsy had discovered a fresh gopher hole near the rim of the canyon by the house, and Ken had tried to flood out the little pest. Evidently he had forgotten to turn off the water, and it had been running all night.

"It's your fault," he told Mugsy, as he turned off the faucet. "Just look at that mess of mud."

Mugsy took the remark as a compliment and tried to lick Ken's cheek. "Don't try to soften me up," Ken protested. "Just because you see my bow and arrows, you needn't think you're going along. No one is allowed to take his dog on the Saturday special."

"Hey, Ken, you ready?" Cubby called from next door.

It was a moment before Ken could locate his friend, perched in an orange tree. "What are you doing up there?" he asked. "Why don't you come on over?"

Cubby chuckled. "I'm watching old Ron and Harvey," he said, "out front trying to get rid of Merv."

Ken said, "They needn't think they're going to bring that bigmouth along."

Cubby dropped down from the tree and gathered up his bow, his quiver, and the marker stick that he had made from his dad's old fishing rod. There was a strip of red cloth tied to the tip end. The stick was used to keep the boys in line on their hunt.

"Don't worry," said Cubby, "they know better than to bring him. They swore to keep the secret same as the rest of us."

Ken took Mugsy in tow and shut him up in the storage room. When he returned, Ron and Harvey came into sight, dragging their feet and trying to ignore Merv, who was right beside them. Merv carried a bow and arrow, which Ken considered a bad sign.

"Where are Vic and Benjie?" he asked, paying no attention to Merv. "Did they decide not to come?"

Harvey looked disappointed. "Vic had to go get his hair cut, and Benjie went to the desert with his folks."

Ron nodded. "Guess we're a little late," he said.

Merv smiled broadly at Ken. "They've been trying to shake me for ten minutes," he explained, "but I stuck like a bandaid."

Ken did not return the smile. "We're just going on a little hike," he said stiffly. "You wouldn't like it."

Merv frowned. "What is this?" he asked impatiently. "Are you guys ganging up on me? Is this Merv's last stand or what?" His searching glance moved from Cubby to Ron to Harvey, but each of them shrugged and gave him the silent treatment. He turned to Ken. "Tell me what's going on," he insisted. "Tell me about this tour of yours that I wouldn't like."

Ken nodded toward the canyon. "We hunt rabbits," he said vaguely.

Merv's eyes took on a stubborn gleam. "Sounds great," he said with false gusto. He pointed to Ron. "His bow is about the right size for a four-year-old, and yet you give me that rabbit routine. Very interesting. Guess I'll tag along. Since the pool's out of bounds, there's nothing else to do."

He backed off, a mocking grin on his face, as though he expected trouble. Ken was sure he and his friends could handle Merv all right, but Mugsy was beginning to howl indignantly from the storage room. At any moment someone in the house would remember something they wanted him to do.

Ken muttered to himself as he turned away. His spirits fell even lower when he saw that the persistent gopher was busy reopening his tunnel. The little pest kept pushing up a fresh mound of earth, exposing his sleek round head as he bobbed in and out. Ken fitted an arrow to his bow and motioned the other boys to stand back out of the way. He was a good shot, and they all knew it except Merv. Silently he crept to the rim of the canyon, took aim, and drew in a deep, steadying breath. Let that head bob up one more time and, zing, that gopher would get it.

Ken was watching the hole so intently that he did not feel the soggy earth tremble under him. Suddenly it gave way. His feet shot out and his arms flung wide as he plunged down the side of the embankment. He descended feet first as speedily as an otter on a mud slide. The breath whooshed out of him as he thumped against a big gray boulder. He lay there fighting for air while sticks and stones and dirt rained down on him. Shaking his head to clear away the fuzzy feeling, he looked up at the top of the embankment. There above him, peering over the grassy rim, were three frightened faces plus Merv's big smile.

"You all right?" Cubby called anxiously.

Slowly Ken got to his feet. He stood on shaky legs, encrusted with mud. "Guess I'm all in one piece," he reported.

"That gopher is sure out to get you," Merv yelled down to him. "How about we start some peace talks?"

There were shouts of laughter as the four came scrambling down the trail. Ken took time out to wipe his hands on a bunch of dry grass. Very funny, he told himself. Listen to those idiots laugh. He had to laugh with them or let Merv show him up as a poor sport.

Cubby gave Ken an affectionate pat on the back. "Nice to have you back on the job," he said with a grin. "You look great wearing that mudpack."

"All right, you jokers," said Ken sternly. "Let's get organized." He took the signal rod from Cubby and handed it to Merv. "You carry the marker and keep to the trail," he said. "The rest of us will fan out and see what we can find."

Merv took the marker reluctantly. "What's the idea?" he protested. "Why can't I fan out too? I'm not going to see anything to shoot if I stay on the trail."

"You have no choice," said Ken. "Keep the red tip high in the air so the rest of us can see it. It's important that none of us get ahead of you."

"That's so no one gets shot," Cubby explained.

"I still don't like it," Merv insisted.

"So we'll take turns," said Ron, who always wanted things to run smoothly.

"We'll meet at the bird's nest," said Ken, pointing far up the canyon to a little white house that seemed to hang out in space. "It's the last house on our side of the canyon," he told Merv.

Merv stood holding the rod, looking uncertain.

"All of you remember we're being watched," Ken warned. "Half the people who live along here are canyon watchers. They keep field glasses handy so they can keep an eye on the wildlife down here."

"Yeah, especially us," said Cubby. "We're the wildest stuff around."

"You know what I mean," said Ken, though he didn't want to say more in front of Merv.

"Sure," said Harvey. "If anyone reports us, we're out of business."

"All right," said Ken. "Shove off."

He and Cubby went out through the brush to the right while Ron and Harvey moved off to the left of the trail. There had been no rain in the area for months, and everything was dry and crackly. A jackrabbit sprang from cover and paused in a little clearing with his nose and ears twitching. Neither Ken nor Cubby gave him a second look. They ranged near and far, stopping to examine every shallow depression in the ground and every hole of any size.

They knew exactly what they were looking for, but they found nothing.

"We should have seen one by now," Cubby said. "Maybe someone squealed on us."

"Sh," cautioned Ken, as he heard a familiar four-note whistle. "Ron and Harvey have spotted something."

They hurried toward the sound of the whistling.

"Over here," Ron called, as they crossed the trail. "I almost stepped on it."

They found him standing beside Harvey. He was staring down at a mess of chicken innards that were all but hidden by a scattering of dirt. Flies hovered over the find, and the sun glinted on metal.

"Another one of those spring-powered traps," said Harvey. "Why don't we get rid of it once and for all?"

"Because it isn't our property," said Ken. "Go ahead, Ron. Trip it."

Ron caught up a stalk of dried yucca and bore down in the center of the bait. It took a couple of thrusts before the circular jaws of the trap snapped shut.

Ken broke off a branch of greasewood. "Move on out," he told the others. "I'll cover our footprints."

He jumped nervously as Merv Hollis peered over a clump of toyon. "So that's what you guys call hunting," Merv said. "Whose trap is that?"

Ken waved him back toward the trail. "We have enough tracks around here," he said. "We don't need any extra ones."

Merv didn't budge. "What kind of a trap is that?" he persisted.

"A coyote trap," Ken said shortly. "You can stand

there asking for trouble all you like, but the rest of us are moving on."

Merv turned away and overtook Cubby and the other boys. "Wait a minute," he insisted. "What's the hurry? Can't I ask a civil question and get a civil answer? Who does that trap belong to?"

Ken made an impatient gesture. "To the exterminator," he said.

"I think he works for the government," Cubby added.

Merv looked genuinely shocked. "You mean to say you guys would destroy government property?" he asked.

Ron shook his head. "We're not destroying anything. It's that exterminator who's trying to destroy every coyote in our canyon. He doesn't care how many pets get caught."

"That's right," said Cubby. "The animals are trapped and left alone to suffer."

Harvey nodded solemnly. "Once we found a dead collie in a trap," he said. "He was half eaten up."

"So now we hunt traps and spring them before they can do any harm," Ron explained.

Merv shook his head in disapproval. "I think that's

pretty stupid. If the government knows there are too many coyotes around here, you ought to leave the traps alone. If you think coyote trapping is wrong, why don't you get up a petition and put a stop to it?"

"It isn't that simple," Ken said. "For one thing, the new people who have bought property along the canyon think coyotes are spooky because they hear them yodel at night. They don't object to the traps."

"And Mrs. Anderson wouldn't sign a petition, because she says a coyote got her best cat," said Harvey.

"Mr. Langley swears a coyote broke into his chicken pen and made off with a big hen," said Ron.

Everyone began to talk at once until Ken shouted for them to pipe down and get on with the hunt. And all the while Merv stood there looking at them as though they were complete idiots.

"You mean to say your folks put you up to messing with these traps?" he asked.

"Of course not," said Ken impatiently. "You think they're stupid?"

"Well, no," Merv said. "But you sure are." Red-faced and angry, he handed the marker to Cubby. "I'm heading back home and I'm willing to bet you someone reports you nuts for messing with government property."

He sounded as if he were threatening them, and the other three boys turned to Ken wondering what they should do. "What about it?" Cubby asked. "Do we quit or fight?"

Ken shook his head and reached for the marker. "Any of you can leave who wants to," he said. "I figure to trip at least three more traps before I sign off."

When he saw that Cubby, Ron, and Harvey were following him, he couldn't resist a parting word to Merv. "Just see to it that you're not the one who reports us," he said.

Merv stood there stiff and annoyed. "I don't scare easy," he said. "I'll report you any time I get ready."

"I wouldn't advise it," said Ken, and he moved on up the trail rather pleased with himself, happy to get rid of old bigmouth.

At least, he had called Merv's bluff and kept his three friends on the job. No doubt about it, you had to stand up to a troublemaker like Merv, or he moved in on you and took over.

THE ALERT

Ken lay in bed and listened to the distant wail of a fire engine. He lifted his head to stare at the clock on his nightstand. A quarter past seven, and it was still rather dark outside.

Boy, smell that smoke. He jumped out of bed and hurried to the open window. Blue sky over the ocean to the west and blue sky to the south, but all was dark overcast to the north.

"Another hot spot must have broken out in Tortugas Canyon," he told himself.

He slipped on his bathrobe and ran downstairs to the kitchen. His mother was busy at the sink juicing oranges. Crissy was setting the table in the breakfast room, and Mugsy was whining and scratching on the back door.

"Morning everyone," he said happily. "I'll bet there's no school today on account of there's a big fire in Tortugas."

"You lose your bet," said Mrs. Marr. "The seven o'clock news reported all schools open for classes except the Tortugas Canyon school."

"Poor old Tortugas gets all the fires," said Ken.

"The fire fighters think they have this one contained," said his mother. "Go back upstairs and put on your slippers. It's too chilly to run around barefooted."

"Shall I let Mugsy in?" Ken asked.

"Not until after breakfast," said his mother.

Ken asked that same question every morning. Although he knew the answer perfectly well, he felt more loyal to Mugsy when he went through the routine.

Upstairs, the bathroom door was open. Mr. Marr stood at the washbasin shaving.

"Did you hear those fire engines last night?" Ken asked. "They were sure whooping it up."

His father smiled at him in the mirror without bothering to turn around. "When you smell smoke, those sirens are sweet music."

"With that fire so near, do you suppose there'll be any school today?" Ken asked.

His father nodded. "Monday through Friday," he said briskly. "Get a move on, or you'll be late."

Ken sighed and went on to his room. He returned to the window and took another look at the sky. Admittedly, it didn't seem any darker than it had when he first got up. He unlatched the screen and stuck out his hand. No wind as far as he could tell. He wet one finger and tried again. There was still not the slightest breeze.

He sighed and began to look for his slippers.

*   *   *

School jogged along as usual. Shortly before noon a dry, hot wind began to blow in from the northeast.

"Feels like a Santa Ana," he told Cubby.

He knew what to expect when he heard a number of sirens wailing in the distance. Three big fire engines came chugging up the hill and passed the school, rattling the windows and rattling the children.

Ken was out on the playground when the principal's voice boomed over the loudspeaker. "Attention all students," he said. "School is dismissed. Go directly home. The Tortugas Canyon fire is out of control. Listen to your radio and television sets for further information regarding the opening of school tomorrow. Do not telephone the school. I repeat, do not telephone the school."

A loud cheer greeted the announcement. Some of the boys and girls were still laughing and horsing around on the school bus when it stopped to let Ken and Cubby and Merv get off. Most of the children figured that canyon fires were just something that parents worried about. Parents saw to it that there were water reservoirs built in the hills, made sure the firebreak trails were kept cleared of brush, and the smart ones kept a broad brush clearance around their house. No harm, the kids figured, in young people enjoying a few fringe benefits such as a half-day session.

"Lots of luck," one of the boys called to Ken, as the bus pulled away. "Maybe the school will burn down."

"Hooray!" yelled a chorus of voices.

Merv scowled at Ken. "Are those kids morons or what?" he asked.

"Aw, they don't mean anything," Ken said. "They just like to make a lot of noise."

"I know what's wrong with you," Cubby told Merv. "You're worried about your dog. Maybe he'll be home by the time you get there. Maybe your folks found him while you were in school."

"What folks?" Merv demanded. "My dad's in New York on a business trip, and my mother's not about to go out beating the bushes for a crazy dog that runs away."

The strange thing about Cubby was that everyone told him their troubles. Ken had not heard about Abdul running away, and yet Cubby must have known all along.

Ken turned to Merv. "Thought you kept Abdul in his run at night," he said.

"I do," said Merv. "But someone must have left the gate open. Either that or he jumped the fence."

"He probably jumped the fence," said Cubby. "Our fence is almost six feet high, and yet the deer get in and chew off the new growth on mother's roses."

Merv pointed ahead at the billows of smoke that boiled up over the distant mountain ridge. The sky was overcast with brownish rusty smoke that bore a heavy acrid smell. Powdery wisps of ash floated in the air.

"I suppose your crazy friends would think it very funny to choke to death on that smoke," he said.

Ken had to remind himself that Merv was a new-comer around here. He caught an ash flake on the palm of his hand and showed it to Merv. "See," he said, blowing on it. "No red edges. They're only dangerous when they show red patches." He brushed the flake away. "We have these scares every year. If there hasn't been any rain, the brush gets tinder dry in the canyons. The minute someone is careless with a match or a cigarette a fire flares up. Don't worry, there're over a thousand fire fighters working on this one. Poor old Tortugas is getting most of the damage."

Cubby said something, but his words were lost in the

thundering roar of a helicopter that beat its way over-head going in the direction of the fire.

"They use those choppers for everything," Cubby yelled above the noise. "They ferry men, lay hose, drop chemicals on the fires, and serve as lookout stations. I'm going to pilot one of those birds someday."

Merv watched the helicopter until it disappeared in the smoke. "All right," he said. "If everything is so safe here in our canyon, why are we sent home from school?"

Ken shrugged. "People get nervous when the radio keeps warning them to be prepared to evacuate their home. I guess they want their kids near them in case they need to make a quick getaway."

Merv began to walk faster. "I'll bet my mother is worried sick," he said.

"Maybe you can quiet her down," said Cubby. "Tell her you've been talking to a couple of old-timers who say our canyon has never had a fire."

He turned to leave them, and Merv paused to stare at the roof of Cubby's house. "What's your father doing up there?" he asked.

Cubby smiled reassuringly. "He's watering down the shingles. Everyone soaks a shingle roof when there's a fire around. Live sparks can start a lot of trouble."

"That's what I thought," Merv said. "We're all sitting ducks."

"You needn't worry," said Ken. "You have a tile roof on your house."

Merv turned away quickly. "I bet you guys don't know what you're talking about."

He hurried on up the hill without a backward glance.

"I'd rather be a sitting duck than a nervous Nellie," said Cubby.

"Where he comes from they only have electric storms and tornadoes," said Ken. "Lots of people go all to pieces when they smell smoke."

Cubby raised a hand in farewell. "Are you going to work Mugsy this afternoon?" he asked.

"Sure," said Ken. "He's doing great."

"I may get to help you," Cubby said doubtfully. "But you know how it is when everyone's glued to the radio."

Ken nodded. "See you later if you can make it," he said.

There was no sign of Bo-the-Crow, but Mugsy came

running to meet him leaving dark footprints in the film of ash that covered the grass. The car was in the driveway, backed in and headed toward the street. And Mr. Marr had the hose going, watering down the sides of the house.

"All right, son, get a move on," he called to Ken. "Get your good clothes and hang them on that rod in the back of the car. You can pack the loose stuff in your suitcase."

Ken stared. "Why are we going to all that trouble?" he asked. "You mean we're actually going to leave our house here all alone?"

"I hope not," said his father. "We'll have to wait and see."

THE SEARCH

The parked car stayed in the driveway all through the night, and Ken slept comfortably in his own bed. Early the next morning he got the aluminum ladder intending to take a look in the tree house to see if he could find any clue to Bo's whereabouts. Bo had not showed up for chow for two days. Ken was worried. In spite of all the trouble Bo caused, he was a favorite pet.

Mugsy came racing up from the side yard and frisked on ahead. As they reached the gate Merv Hollis came running down the road. A pair of binoculars hung from a strap over his right shoulder, and below the glasses he was carrying a canteen that dripped water. His hair was plastered with sweat, his face was streaked with dirt, and his jeans were gray with dust and ashes.

Ken leaned the ladder against the hedge. "What happened to you?" he asked. "Was that you I heard yelling and whistling in the canyon?"

Merv nodded. Wearily he sank down on a lower rung of the ladder. "I'm still looking for Abdul," he said hoarsely. "I kept searching last night until it got too dark to see anything. Then I phoned the dog pound and the police station, but no one had found him. This morning I got up at daylight and started looking again. I've been all up and down the canyon yelling my head off." He reached over and gave Mugsy a friendly pat. "Do you suppose you could get Mugsy to help me?" he asked. "At least, he might pick up Abdul's trail and start me off in the right direction."

Ken's heart swelled with pride. "We might have some luck," he agreed. "Soon as I've had breakfast and we get the news report about school, we'll have a try at it."

Merv bounced to his feet. "Come on," he begged. "I can't wait around. My mother's nervous about the fire. She wants to take off and leave Abdul behind. Come on, Ken, it won't take long. Just get Mugsy to point me in the right direction, and I'll do the rest."

Ken had no intention of going off without leaving word with someone, but Merv grabbed his arm and pulled him along while Mugsy raced on ahead. They hadn't gone more than twenty feet when a green pickup truck came out of the Hollis driveway. The truck paused opposite them while the driver spoke to Merv.

"I left everything watered down," he said. "Cook put the silver service and fancy pieces in the swimming pool, and the missus is sending these special books and paintings down to my place for safe keeping."

The stout woman who sat beside him waved a bulging envelope at Merv. "I forgot to tell your ma I saved the trading stamps," she called.

The truck eased on down the hill. "I'll keep an eye peeled for your dog," the driver called back to Merv. "Don't worry. I'll hurry back and keep things wet down till this fire scare is over."

Merv nodded and waved him on his way. "That's the cook and the gardener," he told Ken. "I'm glad she's gone. She's had the house burned to the ground ever since she smelled the first whiff of smoke."

They found Mrs. Hollis, pale and anxious, sitting in her car with the radio blaring. Someone in a helicopter was reporting on various flare-ups in the burned-over areas. The humidity was down lower than ever, and the chaparral, after two years of drought, was explosively volatile. The observer spoke of fallout, which meant the wind-borne embers, and he spoke of firestorm, the intense fire draft that consumed everything except stone and cement.

Ken saw that Mrs. Hollis had packed her car full of stuff. He stared at what he thought was a bulky two-toned animal until he saw a sleeve and knew that he was looking at two fur coats.

Mrs. Hollis glanced at her wristwatch. "Do hurry," she begged. "I'll give you just half an hour more to look for that dog."

"Don't worry about us," Merv said. "If the fire comes this way, we'll go out on the far side of the canyon."

Mrs. Hollis raised her glasses and dabbed at her eyes with a handkerchief. "Your poor father is going to be frantic when he hears about this fire," she said. "I can't get New York. I can't even get information. The switchboards are jammed."

"Why don't you drive over and talk to my folks?" Ken suggested. "This is old stuff to them."

Mrs. Hollis almost smiled. "That's a good suggestion," she said. "Everyone keeps telling me there's never been a fire in this canyon, but when I'm alone I start to worry."

"Be sure to tell my folks I'll be right back," he said.

"I'll tell them," she promised.

As Ken hurried up the driveway after Merv and Mugsy he saw Mrs. Hollis take a lipstick from her purse, which he felt was a good sign. He and Merv got Abdul's sleeping blanket from the doghouse to take along with them, so they could get Mugsy started off on the right scent. Not until they reached the back

gate, which opened on the canyon, did Ken call Mugsy to him. He kept the dog quiet for a moment before he held the blanket under his nose.

"Seek!" he said sternly. "Seek!"

Mugsy got the idea. He began to sniff around, wandering first in one direction and then in the other.

"I sure hope Abdul didn't go down to the coast highway," said Merv. "If he gets in all that traffic he's a goner."

Mugsy paused and sneezed twice. Then he turned around and retraced his steps heading east up the trail toward the mountains and the billows of dark smoke.

Ken got a spooky feeling as he felt the dry desert wind in his face. "We'd better go back," he said.

"Not yet," Merv urged. "Please, Ken, I've got to find my dog."

Merv had lost his air of cocky superiority. His pleading tone of voice got to Ken who hurried along after Mugsy knowing how he would feel if his own dog were lost.

In the smoky distance ahead of them they heard the sound of hoofbeats and the halooing of men's voices. Presently a band of horses burst out of the haze. Sorrels, bays, palominos, and pintos, all were riderless

and wild-eyed as they snorted and shouldered each other for room on their wild race down the canyon.

They were followed by two horsemen. The one on the right was on a collision course with the boys. At sight of them he let out a yell and reined in his sweat-stained sorrel. The horse sat back in a jolting stop almost on top of Mugsy. The startled dog tucked in his tail and ducked out through the chaparral.

The sorrel high stepped in place, trying to ease the

pull on his reins so he could get back in the race. His
rider scowled down at Ken and Merv. "What the
devil are you kids doing in here?" he demanded.
"Don't you know the whole area is being evacuated?"

"No, sir," said Ken. "We're looking for our dog."

"Did you see a big golden dog?" Merv cried desperately. "I've lost my dog."

"Forget the dog," the man yelled. He made a threatening motion with the coiled reata that he held in his

hand. "Get on out of here before some freak fire turns you into barbecued ribs."

His companion on the far side of the canyon turned in his saddle to shout at him. "Get going, Les. You want to lose the whole bunch on the coast highway?"

One motion of the reins and the sorrel sprang forward, tearing off after the other horses. "You kids get on home," his rider called back. "Them's orders."

"Yes, sir," said Ken, and he began to look around for Mugsy. "Here, boy," he called hurriedly. "Here, boy."

There was no answering bark, no sign of the dog.

"Guess he's still running from that horse," said Merv. "Now we have *two* lost dogs."

Ken was not willing to admit that Mugsy was lost. He was sure his dog had just run on up ahead. Even now Mugsy was probably trying to search out Abdul's trail if there was anything left of it after those horses had messed it up. Ken ran ahead whistling and calling. The smoke was getting worse. It stung his eyes and made the tears run. He stumbled to a halt, and Merv bumped into him. Wordlessly they stared ahead at the reddish glow that appeared in the billows of rusty-colored smoke. The distant wailing of fire-engine sirens seemed to close in from all sides.

"That cowboy was right," Ken said. "We've got to go back."

Smoke tears streaked Merv's cheeks as he scuffed the toe of his shoe in the pebbly dirt. He was unwilling to turn back, and yet he knew they could not go on. "So we're licked," he said.

Ken raised his head and cupped his hand around one ear against the blast of the wind. "Did you hear that?" he cried.

He turned and started running out through the dry, crackling brush toward the sound of Mugsy's excited barking. On the far side of a creosote clump he found his dog circling around Abdul. The golden dog was crouched down in an awkward position with his left forefoot caught in a trap.

Merv bent over him. "Oh, Abdul!" He fell on his knees and cradled Abdul's head in his arms. "Ken, help me get rid of this trap!"

Ken bent closer to examine the dog's blood-caked foot. Abdul flinched and bared his teeth. His rumbling growl warned Ken away.

"Hold him so he can't bite, and I'll get him out of there," Ken said.

Merv clasped both hands around Abdul's muzzle and held on tightly while Ken put his foot on the spring that released the steel jaws of the trap. The moment it opened, Merv pulled Abdul free. Ken tugged out the stake and the chain that held the trap and tossed them into a distant salt bush.

Gently Merv helped Abdul to his feet. The dog stood there trembling and panting. Merv took the canteen from his shoulder and removed the screw cap. Slowly he poured a trickle of water down Abdul's throat.

"I think his leg's broken," Merv said. "Look, he won't put his foot on the ground."

"His whole leg is bound to be numb for a while," Ken said.

Merv looked around desperately. "We've got to get out of here," he said. "D'you suppose we could carry him?"

"He's too big," Ken said. "How about a stretcher? We can tie the corners of his blanket to yucca stalks."

To his dismay, when he started to look around for suitable yucca stalks, Ken saw fierce whirlwinds of fire racing in their direction from the opposite side of the canyon. The fire had circled around the eastern rim and spread to the south. The houses on that side of the canyon stood out like black building blocks against a crimson background. Greedy fingers of flame spilled down the brush-covered slopes. Even as Ken stared, a great ball of fire burst high in the air and sent fire brands sailing his way.

His throat went dry. He couldn't even yell. Mugsy gave a warning yelp as he turned his back on the blast of hot wind and headed for home. Abdul whined and limped after him on three legs.

"Look," Merv cried. "He's going to make it on his own."

"Quick," Ken urged, as he caught up the blanket. "Run for it. We've got to beat that fire to your back gate."

HOT SPOT

Ken and Merv raced after the dogs. The fire from the opposite rim of the canyon created its own fierce draft as it swept from the southeast toward them. In a matter of minutes Ken saw that the fire was sure to beat them to the Hollises' back gate.

The smoke choked him and a pain throbbed in his side as he jogged to a stop and called back the dogs. "The fire's cut us off," he told Merv. "We can't go in the back way. We'll have to climb out here to North Rim Road."

Merv stared at the rim above them where the sky showed nothing but billowy black clouds with a red underglow.

"There's fire over there too," he objected.

"But not so close," said Ken. "It's still in the next canyon. Our best bet is the turnaround at the end of the street. All the brush is kept cleared away."

The stretch of canyon wall above them was steep and rocky. Mugsy managed to struggle up to the top without delay, but Abdul's injured foot got in his way, and he kept pitching forward on his face. The boys had a rough time getting him up the hillside. Merv scrambled ahead and pulled on the dog's collar while Ken braced himself as best he could and boosted the dog from the rear. Ken's hands were bleeding and the smoke had half blinded him by the time they reached the large circular turnaround where North Rim Road ended.

His heart seemed to squeeze shut for one terrified moment as he stared westward toward his own home. The eucalyptus windbreak was a towering whipping mass of flames that shot across the road and licked at the eugenia hedge flanking his driveway. He had known that there was fire to the north, fire to the east, and fire to the south. But now to find the escape route to the west closed filled him with panic.

From where they stood the Hollises' driveway was only a long block away, but the oleander hedge in front of the house was burning, hiding everything behind a pall of oily black smoke. The smoke shifted, and Ken caught a glimpse of the big eucalyptus tree that held the nest of Bo-the-crow. The tree was a crackling inferno. Blazing strips of bark and clumps of burning leaves were flying through the air.

"We're cut off!" Ken had to shout to make himself heard above the roar of the wind. "Fire all around us."

Merv's red-rimmed eyes stared at him in disbelief.

Ken looked around for shelter. The street was deserted. Along this narrow part of the rim most of the houses were built on sturdy stilts. The white frame house to their left belonged to Harvey Bushnell's family. At first Ken thought the Bushnells must have left all the electric lights burning when they were forced to desert their home. Then, right before his eyes, all the windows of the house blew out with a terrific roar, and flames shot out the openings. The overhang at the rear of the house had trapped the driving heat and let the fire eat up from below.

Merv caught his arm and pointed back the way they had come. "No matter what happens, we're lucky to get out of that canyon," he shouted against the wind. "We'd sure be goners if we were in there."

He gave a cry of horror as a cottontail, its coat ablaze, dashed across the road in front of them and threw itself down the hillside, setting off a new trail of fire in the brush.

Ken reached out and flicked a glowing spark from Merv's hair. "Here, we'll use this for cover," he said. He shook out Abdul's woolen blanket and gave Merv a corner. "Hang on," he warned. "The wind's trying to whip it away."

Ken got a firm grip on his corner of the blanket and crowded down beside Merv and the dogs. The dogs were panting and shaking with fright, but they were strangely obedient.

"We can't stay here," Merv protested hoarsely. "We'll roast."

Ken blinked his stinging eyes and tried to peer ahead through the swirls of smoke. Merv was right. The heat was as intense as the blast from an oven. They couldn't just lie there and cook. And yet, where could they go?

"You saw what happened to that cottontail," he shouted.

He wondered how long they could last in this staggering heat. How long before they fell victims to the shower of burning sparks? Must they cower under this smoldering blanket until the fire sucked the very breath from their lungs? Ken buried his face in his arms, trying to ease the agony of that searing heat.

Above the fear was his fury at himself for getting into such a hopeless position. He should never have gone to hunt for Abdul in the first place. "Stupid," he muttered to himself. "Just plain stupid."

Then he felt Abdul pressing against him, trembling and suffering yet quietly trusting. Ken stopped muttering. He had to admit there never was a choice in the first place. He couldn't have left a helpless animal to die in a trap.

Came the moment when the air was too hot to breathe, when his nostrils felt burned raw. Then he heard the distant roar of a big bomber. He was sure it was one of the army planes that had been converted to drop chemicals on hot spots in a fire.

"Listen!" cried Merv.

Above the roar of the fire, above the wailing of distant fire engines, the great throbbing charge of the bomber grew louder and louder.

"Here he comes," Ken shouted hoarsely. "I hope he drops his load on us."

He ducked instinctively as the big plane zoomed in close overhead and, with a swoop, dropped its load of fire-killing solution. For one agonizing moment Ken thought the pilot had overshot the target. But the pinkish mudlike solution doused the worst of the flaming windbreak. The first drop was followed by a second and a third.

Ken got so excited that he jumped to his feet and yelled, "Bull's-eye!"

When the last load of chemicals hit the windbreak, the fire seemed to suck in its breath. Before it could huff and puff to a new start, three fire engines came wailing in through the smoke. The firemen handled the long fat hose with professional skill, sending great streams of water hissing against the blackened boles of the trees. Fire fighters wearing tin hats and laden with back pumps marched in to spray the oleander hedge in front of Merv's house.

A muffled fireman from the smallest truck saw Merv and Ken standing hunched down against the heat. He motioned for them to come closer. "What're you boys doing here?" he demanded sternly.

Ken pointed toward his house. "We live here," he said.

The fireman shook his head wearily. He needed a shave and a shower and a lot of sleep. "Any swimming pools around here?" he asked. "We need extra water."

Shaking with strain, hot tears of relief rolling down his cheeks, Ken ran to lead the way to Merv's pool. Merv and the dogs followed close on his heels.

"This way," Ken told the fireman. "We'll show you."

When the boys reached the Hollises' pool, they dived in clothes and all. Never had anything felt as good as that water under its scum of ash and soot. They sloshed water all over themselves and the dogs while the crew from the fire truck installed their pump. The boys stood by, steaming wet, and watched while the smoldering oleander hedge was watered down again until every last spiral of smoke had disappeared.

Presently, in great haste, all but one of the fire engines used the turnaround to head back west to a new hot spot.

The boys made a quick inspection of Merv's house to make sure it was all in one piece.

"Adobe and tile are the stuff for these canyon houses," Merv said proudly, as though he were an old-timer himself. "No special damage that I can see."

"Come on, let's take a look at my house," said Ken.

They hurried down the road. The smoke was lifting. They could see that Ken's house was still standing. Ken tried to ignore the sinking feeling that pestered him as they came near the group of smoke-blackened men who stood around the one remaining fire truck. After all the women and children had been evacuated under the direction of the police, most of the men had returned home to fight the battle of the rooftops.

"We can call this the miracle of North Rim Road," said one of the men, his voice loud and hoarse.

"That eucalyptus windbreak acted as a firewall," said his neighbor. "It deflected the fire draft and helped save our homes."

"We're lucky the water pressure held up," said Mr. Conners, Cubby's father, "and that those bombers got here in time."

Mr. Marr nodded. "Good thing I was holding on to the TV antenna with one hand when they came over or I'd have been sucked off the roof," he said. "Those pilots are tops. . . ." He paused and stared as Ken and Merv approached with the subdued dogs close on their heels. "What are you doing here?" he demanded. "Merv, your mother said you were taking the dogs out on the far side of the canyon."

Ken could see his father was shocked and angry. "No, sir," he said quickly. "That was our emergency plan. But it didn't work. You see, we couldn't find Merv's dog, and a bunch of horses came crashing down the canyon and ruined his trail. Then when we found him, he was caught in a coyote trap. It took us a long time to get going."

"Ken, of all the foolish things! You might have been killed. Well, we'll talk about it later. Right now I've got to take another look at our roof." His teeth looked extra white in his smoke-stained face as he smiled at Ken and gave him a big bear hug. "Do me a favor, son," he said. "See if you and your friends can stay out of trouble for five minutes."

"We'll stick around close," Ken promised.

Cubby's father started off toward his own house, but he paused and turned back as though he had remembered something important.

"Saw your crow over on the golf course yesterday," he told Ken. "He ruined my drive from the seventh tee with that 'What's new?' squawk of his. Birds are the first to leave a threatened area, you know; but they always return. Guess I'd rather have Bo steal my car keys, though, than ruin my golf score."

Ken heaved a quivery sigh of relief. "Thanks for telling me, Mr. Conners. I was sure worried about Bo."

Mr. Conners nodded and went on his way.

Merv turned to Ken. "So old Bo-the-crow will still be with us?" he said, smiling.

Ken thought it just as well to change the subject. "No wonder I feel all gone," he said. "I'm starved. I'm going home and cook myself bacon and eggs and drink cold milk till it runs out my ears."

Merv asked an odd question. "Is your stove gas or electric?"

He had to nod toward the two burned out electric-power poles across the road before Ken got the idea.

"It's an electric stove," he admitted.

"Let's go to my house," Merv said. "If there's no gas, we can use charcoal in the barbecue pit." He looked at Ken with a solemn smile. "You're welcome to anything at my house," he added. "Anything at all."

He turned away quickly as though he were em-barrassed by his offer of friendship. Ken stood there and tried to take everything in. Gradually he under-stood that Merv actually wanted him to know he was welcome at the big house. Ken drew in a deep, satisfying breath. He began to wonder where he had left his swim trunks. Something told him that before long he would be back on his favorite slide in his favorite pool. *Zowie! Splash!* He could see himself swimming the full length of the pool, and all underwater.

How such a frightening morning could make so many changes was hard to understand. Still, he knew now that Merv was a good one to have along in an emergency and he was glad to be his friend.

"Soon as we eat," he said, "how's about we take a look at the pool? We may as well start cleaning up out there."

Merv nodded. "We'll do that," he said. "But first we eat."

"First we eat," Ken agreed. "There's no hurry. No hurry at all."